The Space Between

The Space Between

KATE SMITHSON

www.anongray.com

THE SPACE BETWEEN

Copyright © 2023 by Kate Smithson

Kate Smithson, Seattle, WA

The Space Between

www.anongray.com

Library Of Congress Control Number: 2023901720

ISBN (paperback): 979-8-218-13541-6

First Edition: February 2023

Illustrations copyright © shutterstock.com/Tithi Luadthong

Printed in the United States of America

For Ben

BEACON HILL
COMMUNITY COLLEGE

December 17, 2005

Dear Aada,

It is with regret that the Philosophy Department at Beacon Hill Community College terminates your employment effective January 1, due to your repeated tardiness and absences. We've attempted to support you during your health crisis by offering extended sick leave, use of vacation time, and a paid sabbatical. Six months later, you are still unable to return to work consistently.

Recently, we've discussed your future with our institution but you have been uncooperative. Most recently you received a written warning on November 1. In that warning I again reminded you of our policies and departmental procedures regarding attendance.

You may contact me at 206-347-9212 to arrange a time to return your keys and collect any personal items left in your workplace. You may contact Amy Whitman, Benefits Specialist, at 206-347-7844 to discuss your benefits options. You may contact, Judy Snyder, Employee Relations Director at 206-347-3650 with any other questions you may have.

Sincerely,

Margot L Chambers

Margot L. Chambers
Department Chair

By my signature below, I hereby acknowledge that I received a copy of this notice of discipline. My signature does not necessarily indicate agreement with the contents.

Aada Talbot

Aada Talbot, December 28th, 2005

1

Every bus passenger had a story.
Most of the time they poured out unprompted. A
disembodied voice would float up from behind Evelyn's seat
as she drove, recounting a story wilder than fiction.
Sometimes it was a story of triumph (celebration likes an
audience). Other times it was a story of struggle (misery
prefers company). Every one of them was captivating.

Evelyn's friends and family back home in Louisiana often
asked her why she chose to drive a bus in dreary Seattle. Her
education had prepared her to do prestigious things, and she
was born and raised in the sun! But Evelyn loved her route,
and the rain for that matter. From uptown to downtown, she
indulged in real-life stories far more engaging than any
Netflix drama, all against a backdrop of greens and blues.

Most of Evelyn's riders were regulars, at least in this part
of the city. They were often loud and outspoken about the
hard times they faced. Evelyn did what she could to help
them smile, even if only to watch their faces drop as they
stepped off the bus.

Today was no different. The road was loud. Puddles
splashed violently beneath the bus as Evelyn drove past tall

buildings, strip malls, and vacant lots. Highways crossed above and below one another. Steam billowed from manholes as if they were harboring dragons.

The heat was on full blast, and the passenger's windows were fogged over with a layer of condensation so thick the road was completely obscured. They could have been anywhere— anywhere it rained.

"Next stop, 145th and Main," Evelyn announced. "Be sure to get your umbrellas ready, folks. It's raining out there!" She let out a little chuckle as she turned her attention to the front door. "Good morning, good morning, good morning!" she crooned as passengers boarded her bus. "Y'all looks like a bunch of drowned rats! Jody, where's your umbrella? Get in here. You'll catch a cold! Mark, did you make it to that sale at the Dollar Store? I told you it was good! Hi ya, Sandi. Hang on, let me lower this bus for you. I've been telling you to get to the doctors about that ankle." Evelyn prided herself on knowing exactly what to say to make someone feel seen and loved.

Evelyn moved to close the doors when she was startled by a figure in the rain. A woman stood transfixed, staring into the bus, feet glued to the sidewalk. Her thin, dark hair was plastered to her scalp by the downpour, and her cheeks were cut with deep grooves. Her eyes were piercing blue and her lips were cracked and scabbed over in parts. She wore a trench coat that, from what Evelyn could tell, had been beige at one point, but was now more of a mottled brownish grey. It hung open, despite the rain, exposing the mid-length jumper and tattered pantyhose that sagged at the knees and ankles. On her feet were a pair of dress flats with holes that revealed the woman's pinky toes.

"Well hi there, hon! You getting on board?" Evelyn asked. The woman hesitated, but then boarded. She pulled her trench coat tight as she entered the warm, dry bus, but not before Evelyn noticed her collarbone jutting out like a hanger. "Sweetheart, you are just skin and bones under there. You eating all right?"

Without a word the woman looked down at the toll box. Water dripped off the ends of her hair as she reached into her pocket to retrieve some coins. They jangled in the empty space between them. Evelyn glanced at the woman's hands. Hints of a manicure gone long ago danced around her cuticles against a backdrop of caked-on dirt and grime. The woman flinched when she noticed Evelyn's gaze and pulled her hands back into her sleeves as she moved toward the back of the bus. But the bus was bulging at the seams on account of all the rain. The only spot left was immediately behind Evelyn.

Evelyn checked her rear-view mirror before pulling out into traffic. No one spoke. The only sound was that of water splashing against the bus and hot air pumping through the vents. Some people napped. Others checked their phones and tried to stay awake. The entire bus seemed to struggle to pull itself through the oppressive weather. *Such a pity*, Evelyn thought to herself. *Morning's the best time to be alive! And the rain? Well, that's the reason everything's lush and—*

Evelyn's thoughts were interrupted by a voice coming from behind her: "Sure seems like the rain will never stop."

It's that woman from the bus stop, isn't it, Evelyn thought. The voice was coarse, and reminded her of her grandmother who died of emphysema. Evelyn adjusted her posture and craned her neck to see past the edges of her rear-view mirror. "Don't I know it, sweetheart!" Evelyn replied. "Makes my bus all messy. Takes ages to get her clean again."

Then silence.

"It's a shame, really," the voice continued after a few moments. "It makes me think of my sister."

"Oh? How old's your sister?" Evelyn asked, doing her best to pace herself. She didn't want to take up all the space with her own words.

"She's seven years younger than me, and it's February now, so I guess that would make her 23."

Evelyn was desperate to see the woman's face. She fidgeted with her rear-view mirror again, but all she could see was a pair of scuffed, nylon-covered knees. It didn't help that everything was vibrating with each bump of the bus.

"She's pretty irresponsible," the voice continued.

Exasperated, Evelyn let go of the mirror and decided to just listen.

"We've lived here for ages, but she can never remember to bring an umbrella."

"Oh, Lord." Evelyn replied. "That sounds about right. Little sisters, am I right? But they're not all bad, are they?"

From behind her seat, Evelyn heard a half-hearted "Yeah." Then silence.

Evelyn was getting frustrated. *How on Earth am I supposed to have a conversation with someone if I can't see their face?* She had half a mind to stop the bus in the middle of the street so she could turn around and look this woman in the eye. *Evelyn, sweetheart*, she crooned to herself. *No amount of eye contact will make or break it for this woman. Just be available.* Evelyn let out a heavy sigh.

"Do you know where I can get an umbrella?" the women asked. "Maybe I'll get one for my sister, you know, for old time's sake."

Evelyn's heart skipped a beat. As much as she enjoyed hearing stories from her riders, what she loved most was being helpful. "Well, there's the Dollar Store, or Goodwill probably has some. You could try one of those outdoor shops. I bet they've got some pretty nice ones, not that I think it makes much of a difference. When rain goes sideways, it doesn't matter how expensive your umbrella is: you're going to get wet." Evelyn let out a gregarious laugh. Humor always helped put people at ease.

"That's a good idea. Thanks," the woman said. Evelyn pictured the woman's smile. And just like that, the flood gates opened: "It was my little sister's birthday a month ago. We used to have this running joke: I'd buy her an umbrella for her birthday, and I swear she'd leave it at home just to provoke me. Man, did we argue over the stupidest things, too. We could never figure out how to get along. My mom and dad would always say, 'You two are like oil and vinegar. You have trouble coming together, but when you do, it's delicious.'" The woman paused, then continued: "I think about her a lot. We don't really talk anymore. Not since our parents died and things went sideways." And then, as abruptly as the words came, they stopped.

Evelyn's mind filled with questions. *No talking at all? What happened between them? Wouldn't her little sister want to know what's become of her big sister? Are there no other family or friends to care for this woman?* Evelyn tried to fit the pieces of the story together in her mind. Something about this woman stirred up an uneasy feeling in Evelyn's gut.

Whether she cared to admit it or not, Evelyn's cheerful exterior was more armor than optimism. It was a matter of self-preservation. Like everyone else, Evelyn had her own set of problems. Getting too close to her demons, by way of other people's stories, had a sobering effect.

"My name's Aada," the woman said, interrupting Evelyn's thoughts.

Evelyn responded as cheerfully as she could: "Oh! Hello, Aada. That's a lovely name. I'm Evelyn. I'm sorry to hear about your sister and your parents. How long has it been?"

"What, since my parents died, or since I last talked to my sister?"

"Either."

For a long time, neither woman spoke. Evelyn wondered if she had crossed an invisible boundary.

The next bus stop was in sight. Evelyn resumed her bubbly demeanor as she announced to her passengers, "We're coming up to University Ave. Get your umbrellas out, folks. It's coming down out there!"

A mass of young students waited anxiously at the bus stop. Some stood under umbrellas, but mostly they were too cool to acknowledge the rain. Evelyn chuckled as she noticed a few students using their hands to squeegee their faces. "Oh, Lord." Evelyn called back to Aada, "Would you look at what we have here, Aada?" Evelyn couldn't help but roll her eyes in good humor. Students were a unique breed.

The doors opened, and Evelyn glanced through her rear-view mirror to check for Aada's response. Only Aada's knees were no longer in sight. Evelyn craned her neck to get a better look at the back of the bus just in time to watch Aada slip out the rear door. Evelyn's body sank deep into her chair. *Hon,* she told herself, *don't give it a second thought. You'll see her again. Have patience.*

Evelyn closed her eyes and mouthed a little prayer: "Lord, please help Aada find what she's looking for." Then she turned her attention to the oncoming passengers. "Good morning! Good morning, folks! Let's get y'all out of that rain."

Evelyn looked for Aada along sidewalks and at bus stops for weeks after that day, but she never saw her again. Eventually she had to make her peace with the small scrap of story Aada had gifted her with, but not before purchasing an umbrella to keep on the bus just in case she saw Aada again.

2

Luca stood in the rain waiting for the bus, a ball of irritation surrounded by undergrads in Gore-Tex jackets or hiding beneath waterproof umbrellas. Her wool peacoat and leather clogs may have looked professional, but they weren't the best at keeping out the rain.

She wished she hadn't left her umbrella back at her apartment. *Stop beating yourself up, Luca! At least you're not an undergrad anymore,* she told herself as she glanced around. Her own graduation had been two months ago, but it felt like a lifetime. She didn't bother to attend the ceremony. No one would have come anyway. It didn't matter. She'd earned a *paid* internship with the Fred Hutchinson Center. Science was her family now, a far less disappointing relative than any of her actual ones.

The bus careened toward the curb, sending a tidal wave of water onto the sidewalk. Luca jumped back. *Yeah, like that's going to make a difference,* she thought. She couldn't help but laugh at herself. The mass of lethargic students began shuffling onto the bus. Luca casually glanced at the stream of people leaving through the back door. For a split second she saw someone who reminded her of her older sister. Squinting in the rain, Luca called out to the woman: "Aada?" The woman didn't respond and Luca decided she was just seeing things. After all, Aada would never be caught dead without an umbrella in the rain. Luca could feel a coolness creeping into her thoughts. Her sister, Aada, was notorious for making Luca feel like life was harder than it needed to be.

As Luca boarded the bus her favorite bus driver, Evelyn, greeted her: "Good morning, Luca, or should I say, Hi, drowned rat?"

Luca giggled in spite of herself. "Hey, Evelyn."

"What happened? Did your umbrella dump you again?"

"Nope. He's patiently waiting for me at home."

"Maybe he'll do some dishes while he's there!" And then it came, a laugh that made the whole bus shake. Luca was convinced that Evelyn's laugh could cure far more diseases than anything she'd ever discover in a lab. Her bus driver's joy was infectious.

"Thanks for the laugh, Evelyn. You always help me start the day right."

"Just doing my job, hon. Just doing my job."

Luca headed to the back of the bus, popped her earbuds in, and began daydreaming the city blocks away. Only this time her daydreams weren't about winning Nobel Prizes or meeting mister or misses right. They were dreary and grumpy, full of thoughts about her sister, whose memory she hadn't entertained in months. *Why today?* Luca thought. It didn't matter. Now that Aada was in her head, she'd be there all day.

Luca couldn't help but run down the list of grievances her sister was responsible for, the worst being when Aada sold their family house after their parents died in a car accident. Luca vowed to never speak to her sister after that, but it stung even more to see Aada act so cool about it all. They were her parents too, after all. All Luca had ever wanted was to have a friend for a sister, maybe even a mentor. And after their parents died, she really hoped they could support one another. Instead, her big sister had taken a clinical approach to keeping in touch. "Pff. Love, my ass." Luca said under her breath.

The person sitting in front of Luca turned around and scowled. "Do you mind?"

Luca looked down at her foot banging against the seat in front of her. "Sorry," she mouthed, and returned to staring out the window.

Getting off a few blocks from her lab, Luca shouted, "See you tonight, Evelyn!" as she headed through the back door. Luca couldn't make out what Evelyn shouted back, but assumed it was a joke, as the woman's laughter followed her out of the bus doors.

Luca checked her watch and decided there was enough time for a cup of coffee. She headed into her favorite indy coffee shop. Good coffee on every corner of the city was of small consolation for the months of clouds and rain. Still, she smiled as she rounded the corner and saw the shop sign greeting her. The inside smelled of old books and coffee grounds, cinnamon and wet dog. Squishy chairs and couches were scattered like dice, and there was a wall covered from floor to ceiling with books and magazines. This was Luca's happy place.

Unfortunately Luca was too deep in thought to hear her favorite barista say hello to her. Happy place or not, Luca was out of sorts. Her sister had gotten into her head and it was proving to be a real struggle to get her out. Luca collected her coffee and picked up a copy of *Emu Today & Tomorrow*. She sat on one of the sepia-colored couches and tried to remember the last time she had received a voicemail from her sister. *It must have been three or four weeks now.*

Luca checked her call history and scowled. *How could Aada not call for four months? Has she given up on me?*

Luca would be lying if she said she didn't secretly love listening to Aada's weekly voicemails. Of course Luca never picked up when her sister called, but it was still nice to know someone cared about her. Aada was a difficult person to deal with, but she was all the family Luca had left. To entertain the idea of being forgotten was too much. Luca began to tear up. *It's one thing to live and work alone. It's another thing to be alone.* She missed being part of a family.

Luca ached for a hug, or to punch a wall. It was hard to understand her feelings. She dabbed at her eyes as she recalled the last words she had yelled at her sister: "I'll never speak to you again!" If Luca was anything, she was stubborn. *Arg! Why hasn't Aada called?*

Luca imagined what she'd say to her sister if she called: "Hey, Aada. It's me, Luca, *your sister.* Haven't heard from you for a while. I'm fine by the way. Thanks for caring."

Then she heard her sister's monotone voice in her head: "Oh. Hi, Luca. Sorry, I've been busy. So...what have you been up to?"

"Well, I graduated top of my class *two months ago*, and landed a great internship. It's paid and could turn into a real career if I do well."

"Uh-huh...great. So you must be getting out of that dingy studio apartment then?"

"My apartment's fine, Aada. Just because I still live in the U-district doesn't mean I'm failing at life. God, you can be such a snob."

"Geez, Luca. Why are you freaking out? You called me, remember?"

"Yeah, because you haven't picked up the phone in four months! That's a third of a year, *Aada*. I thought being sisters meant something to you!"

A customer sitting alone by Luca cleared his throat and peered at her over his glasses.

Luca realized she'd been having her hypothetical conversation with Aada out loud. She glanced around and noticed more than one startled customer. "Sorry. Sorry, everyone." Luca felt her face blush and she slumped low into the cushions. "Enough is enough," she said to herself under her breath. Luca reached for her phone and called Aada for the first time in a year.

"You've reached Aada Talbot. Please leave me a message and I'll get back to you as soon as I can. Thanks."

Figures. Luca stuffed the phone into her messenger bag and tossed her copy of *Emu Today & Tomorrow* onto the couch. Luca looked up at the clock on the wall. She would have preferred to drink her coffee at the shop, but there was a limit to how late she could arrive to work and still feel good about cashing her paycheck. She stood up and nearly tripped over the tattered carpet, barely catching her coffee, as she stumbled toward the glass door. *Damnit! This is always how it goes. Why does she have to be like this? What did I ever do to her?*

"Thank you! See you tomorrow!" she called to the barista as she headed out the door.

"Bye, Luca," the barista replied.

The day was clearly going to be a wash. The next 18 hours flashed before Luca's eyes: Go to work distracted and grumpy; leave feeling despondent and put-out; head home and eat an entire chocolate cake after a dinner of cereal and milk; shut off the phone so Aada could get a taste of her own medicine; wrap up in a blanket while binge watching reruns of *Friends* till the wee hours of the morning; and regret it all when I sleep through my alarm and arrive to work late the next day.

Luca pushed the cafe door open wide and caught the lip of the door jam with her foot. "Damnit!" *Yep,* Luca thought as she stumbled on broken bits of sidewalk on her way to the lab, *it's going to be one of those days, and it is definitely Aada's fault.*

She steadied her cup of coffee and readjusted her messenger bag. From the corner of her eye, Luca noticed a woman in a quilted jacket watching her. She was sitting against a cement planter and had a garbage bag wrapped around her shoulders. The hair peeking out from under her knit cap was reddish-brown and curly. Their eyes locked and Luca mustered a smile. The woman gestured to a small piece of cardboard lying in front of her that read: "Hungry and homeless. Anything helps. God bless." Luca checked her pockets for loose change. As she dug deeper, the cup in her other hand slowly tipped and emptied coffee down the length of her jacket and into her clogs. "No, no, no! Shit! Seriously?!"

The woman sitting against the cement planter chuckled and said, "Maybe the rain will wash it off."

"Yeah. Maybe," Luca replied. She focused on steading the empty cup in one hand as she resumed her search for loose change with the other. But all that she had was some balled- up tissues and a stick of used lip gloss. Luca gave a feeble smile to the woman and mouthed "Sorry" as she gestured to her empty pockets.

The woman flashed a toothless grin at Luca. "That's all right. Have a nice day."

The rain came down harder. To avoid further interaction, Luca reached for her phone to check the time. *Shit! Now I'm really late!* Luca cinched the belt on her jacket, dropped the empty coffee cup into a nearby garbage can and started running the three blocks to her lab.

"Hey, Lady!" The woman sitting on the sidewalk called after Luca. "You should get yourself an umbrella!"

3

Jude tried to get comfortable. The sidewalk was cold and hard, but she'd been lucky enough to snag a quilted jacket from a coat drive. At least her top half was warmish. She adjusted her sign and tried making herself look approachable. The cafe Jude sat outside of was extra busy on this cold February day. The door was in constant motion. Jude inhaled deeply; the smell of caffeine made her feel warm. As much as she liked the idea of having something warm to drink, she would have felt warmer knowing someone missed her.

Jude looked up at the cloudy sky. A few tiny raindrops fell on her face. *Don't you start raining for real.* She had a few garbage bags with her that kept her mostly dry, but the rain was still a real bummer for someone living on the streets like her. She could feel herself starting to gripe and knew if she continued it would be a downward spiral of doom. She tried turning her mood around: *I may not have much, but I'm glad for what I do have.*

Jude scanned the sidewalk in hopes of catching a friendly expression. A woman wearing a worn-out trench coat was staring into the cafe window. Poking out from beneath the jacket were a pair of ragged dress flats and some tattered nylons. Jude cocked her head. Was this woman waiting for someone to come out? *Nah,* Jude thought. *Folks like us don't know folks that go into places like that.*

Jude called out to the woman: "Hey, lady. You looking for someone?" No acknowledgement. Jude tried again, a little louder: "Hello? Do you need to use the bathroom or something?" Nothing. "If you wait at the bathroom door, you can catch it when someone's coming out. Then you don't have to ask for the key."

The woman shot a look of disgust at Jude.

"Well, excuse me for trying to be helpful." It wasn't the first time Jude had been so aggressively dismissed, but that didn't make it any less painful.

Jude looked the woman up and down and noticed she was holding a brand-new umbrella still in its plastic sleeve. "Hey. You plan on using that umbrella? It's not raining sunshine you know." Jude laughed. Her voice crackled. Decades of smoking to stay warm had left her voice tired and weathered.

"It's not for me."

Jude was surprised by the woman's reply and pressed on: "My name's Jude. What about you, Umbrella Lady? You got a name?"

"Aada Talbot," the woman replied, still glued to her spot in front of the cafe window. "Is that your real name?"

The woman turned to face Jude. "You asked me my name, didn't you? It's Aada Talbot."

"Don't you know anything?" Jude motioned for the woman to come closer. "You've got to protect your identity! Don't call attention to yourself like that, and definitely don't go around flaunting your real name. What if the cops come and say, *Hey, have you seen a lady named Aada Talbot?* Now I'm going to have to tell them I have! Better get yourself a nickname. Then no one has to worry about getting anyone into trouble. If the cops say, *Hey, have you seen a lady named Aada Talbot?* I can say, *Nah. Never met anyone by that name.* See?"

The woman stared at Jude without blinking.

"Hellooo? Earth to Umbrella Lady. Did you hear me?" Either the woman was confused by what Jude had said, or she thought Jude was crazy.

After a bit, the woman spoke through clenched teeth: "I'm nothing like you."

"All right. Geeze. No need to get bent out of shape. Just trying to be helpful. Damn."

The woman stepped away from Jude and turned back to the cafe. A gust of wind tossed leaves and discarded napkins into the air.

Jude pulled her quilted jacket up around her chin and shook water droplets off her shoulders. She pulled out a garbage bag and wrapped it around herself.

The noise made the woman flinch and she glared in Jude's direction.

"Sorry. Didn't mean to startle you, your majesty." Jude was used to getting attitude from people, but she still felt sorry for this woman. Umbrella Lady seemed out of sorts and she wasn't like the other folks Jude knew from the shelters. "If you're not planning on opening that umbrella, you could come share a garbage bag with me. I've got extra." Jude made space on her piece of cardboard.

"I'm fine. I was about to leave anyway."

"Suit yourself, Umbrella Lady." Jude smiled at the woman. "Hey, if you want, there's a good spread at the shelter on Pine. If you're lucky, there might even be a spot at the Evergreen Women's Shelter tonight. It's just up the road from there. Get there early. With all this rain, there's likely to be a line."

"Thanks. But again, I'm fine."

"Suit yourself, but they've got clean bathrooms and they keep the lights on at night."

The woman shot daggers at Jude. "I'm fine!" Any friendliness had drained from her face. Then, spooked by something, the woman collected herself and dashed across the street.

"See you later, Umbrella Lady!" Jude could barely finish her sentence before the woman disappeared around the corner. *Man, I remember that. Feeling so confused, like you've been plunked down on an alien planet, and the way people look through you. Makes you wonder why you were ever born. Sucks.* Jude rarely allowed herself a moment to remember her own journey to the streets. She couldn't dwell on the past too long. It was too depressing. She shook the thoughts out of her head and turned her attention to the corner where the woman had disappeared. *Ah, Umbrella Lady's going to be all right. Jude's got her back, even if she doesn't realize it yet.* Jude smiled.

The doors of the cafe flew open and a young woman tumbled out, wearing a camel colored peacoat, grey tights, and black clogs. She slung a messenger bag over one shoulder and held a coffee in her other hand. The woman locked eyes with Jude and proceeded to check her pockets for change. But while one hand dug around in her pocket, the other slowly emptied the contents of her cup down her jacket. "No, no, no! Shit! Seriously?!"

Jude chuckled. *Karma's a bitch, huh.* Instantly she regretted how mean-spirited her thoughts were. "Maybe the rain will wash it off," she called to the woman.

"Yeah. Maybe." The woman dug around in her pockets some more, then flashed a sheepish smile. "Sorry."

"That's all right. Have a nice day." More than pity, Jude hated the guilty looks she was given. *Guilt never does anybody any good.* Her caseworker had taught her that. *It just leaves us both feeling bad. Just ignore me if that's the way you're going to be.* The drizzle turned into drops and the drops quickly turned into a deluge.

The young woman with the coffee down her jacket took off toward the hospital. Jude watched as she stumbled on the uneven cement. Shaking her head, she called out, "Hey, lady! You should get yourself an umbrella!"

Jude was used to the rain, but even she had her limits. Water was getting in through the creases of her well-worn garbage bags and the ends of her curls were dripping cold water down her neck. "Enough's enough." She mumbled to herself. "I can only take so much rain." She hated giving up her spot in front of the cafe but the warm dry shelter was calling her name. She packed up her things and set her sights on the watered down coffee and the day old bagels waiting for her.

Jude decided to take a short cut through the park. At least it was a little dryer than out on the sidewalk. The volunteers were setting out the last tray of sandwiches as she arrived. "Perfect." Jude smiled. She squelched over to the folding tables covered in food and grabbed a sandwich wrapped in a plastic baggie, a bright-red apple, and a bottle of water. "Thanks!" she said to the volunteer.

Seven round conference tables sat scattered around the room with six blue plastic chairs at each. The walls were decorated with posters advertising clean needle exchanges, help for victims of domestic violence, and safety rules for the shelter. Jude scanned the room for an empty spot when she noticed Aada, the Umbrella Lady from in front of the cafe, sitting all alone. Jude wandered over to the table and sat down. "Hey," she said. "Funny seeing you here."

Aada looked up at Jude and rolled her eyes as she stuffed a large bite of sandwich into her mouth. Her hair was messier than Jude remembered, and she wasn't wearing saggy pantyhose anymore. Instead she had a pair of grey sweat pants on under her trench coat that looked as if they were three sizes too big.

"Look," Jude continued. "I'm sorry if I upset you. I was just trying to be helpful. I haven't seen you around here before. You from out of town?"

Aada narrowed her eyes as Jude sat down next to her. "I grew up around here," Aada replied. "But it's my first time *here*."

"Yeah. You didn't look familiar."

Aada sighed. "No. I imagine not."

"What were you doing at that cafe?"

"My little sister was in there."

"Hold on. Your sister was inside? Why didn't you go in and talk to her?"

Aada stared at Jude. "Look at me! Besides, she's better off without me."

Jude paused. "Don't you think she would have liked seeing her sister?"

"Honestly, Jude, no. We kind of had a falling out a while back."

"I'm listening," Jude said as she folded her arms on the table.

Aada rolled her eyes. "When our parents died I sold our house. My sister—her name's Luca—vowed she'd never forgive me. Then she walked out of my life."

"Damn."

"It's fine. We never got along. Not as kids or adults. Our parents dying just added one more rift between us. Maybe it was just a matter of time before one of us walked away. Besides, from what I could tell, she's doing okay. Better than me, that's for sure."

Jude was touched; it took guts to show vulnerability, especially out here. "Look. I can't fix what happened to you, but if you want some company, I'm around."

"Thanks. It's been a long time since I had a friend." Aada sipped at her cup of tea. "Sorry about how rude I was."

"Nah. That's all right. Jude's a strong gal." Jude put her hand on Aada's shoulder and smiled. "Well, I think that's enough depressing stories for one day. What do you say we check out the desserts!?" Jude knew there was little value in dwelling on the past; it just kept folks from figuring out what to do next.

4

Rhonda leaned back in her chair in a huff. She pulled her brown hair back and snapped it tight with a rubber band. She wasn't spiteful, per se. Mostly she was tired. Trying to help broken people was like riding a rollercoaster through a haunted house, and Rhonda wasn't as young as she once was. Recently she'd noticed her nerves beginning to fray. She was wound tight and her volatile disposition bothered her. Sure, there were days when she smiled, emboldened by the faded sign taped to her wall that read, *Tomorrow I Will Save The World.* But most days the system won and left her exhausted.

Rhonda checked her phone. Five minutes till my next appointment. No file had been created for this new client. It was unclear how long the client had been struggling, or what she hoped to get out of this meeting. According to the small note Rhonda had been handed, the woman had recently started utilizing the meal programs provided by the shelter. That was all Rhonda knew: Female. Hungry.

Rhonda heard someone clear their throat just outside her office door. She looked up and saw a woman she didn't recognize standing in the doorway. "Can I help you?" Rhonda asked.

"I'm Aada. Are you Rhonda?"

"Why yes, I am. I was just about to come find you, Aada. Come on in." Rhonda held out her hand. She liked to use a handshake as a way of reading a person's emotional state.

Some clients saw it as offensive or condescending. Others saw it as a sign of respect and equanimity. And then there were those individuals who were so disgusted by her naive optimism in a cold and cruel world that they practically spit on her hand.

Aada reached for Rhonda's hand and squeezed it tightly. The slightest smile flashed across her face.

Rhonda smiled back. *I just might make an impact today.* "Why don't you take a seat." Rhonda gestured to the two chairs on the opposite side of her desk. "So, Aada, am I pronouncing that right?" Aada nodded. "I wasn't given much information about you. But I'm guessing since you're here, you're looking for some help. Why don't you start by tell me a little bit about yourself."

Aada couldn't seem to get comfortable. She perched on the edge of her seat, back erect, arms rigid, hands firmly pressed against her knees. "I'm not sure how to begin, except that I know I need a job."

Rhonda was used to her clients getting straight to the point. There was a certain level of urgency that came with living on the edge, but there was something unique in Aada's tone. Her resolve seemed grounded and resolute. It took Rhonda by surprise. "Well, what kind of work are you looking for?"

"Something in higher education, ideally."

Rhonda raised an eyebrow and searched Aada's face for a sign she was joking, but the woman was dead serious. Rhonda cleared her throat. "Okay. Can you tell me why that particular field?"

"I used to teach philosophy at Beacon Hill Community College."

"Really? Why not go back and teach there?"

"Things didn't end on great terms with them, so I'm looking to start at a different college, or maybe even a university."

Rhonda leaned forward to make sure she was hearing things right. She looked Aada in the eye. Rhonda had heard some tall tales before, but this one took the cake. Still, she tried to remain professional. She'd gone into social work at the Evergreen Women's Shelter because she was passionate about helping women who found themselves in a vulnerable state, and that meant she had to keep an open mind. "Aada, I think that's a great goal, but maybe let's start by making sure your basic needs are met first. Can you tell me how you wound up in my office?"

Aada looked out the window and sighed, all her resolve gone in an instant. "I'm not sure what happened, just that all the people I loved were there one day, gone the next. Things sort of spiraled out of control, and now, I'm here with you."

"What do you mean when you say all the people you loved are gone?"

"They're just gone. That's all."

Rhonda sensed Aada's resistance to sharing her story. Maybe the details were blurry. Aada started rubbing the sides of her head. She had a pained look on her face. "Do you have any lavender oil?" she asked. "I've had the worst headaches lately. Just yesterday I practically threw up it hurt so bad."

"You're in luck! It just so happens that I do. I use an oil diffuser in here sometimes." Rhonda pulled a bottle of lavender oil out of her desk drawer and offered it to Aada. She watched as Aada put a few drops on her palms and rubbed it on her temples. "Would you like some Tylenol, Aada? I have that too."

"Oh, no. I don't take drugs."

Rhonda smiled. "Sounds good."

"Now, why couldn't my girlfriend accept that?" Aada said indignantly.

"I'm sorry? What do you mean?"

"Nothing. I just think it's nice when people don't try to force someone to take some pill they obviously don't need. Other people in this world could learn from you."

"Is that right?" Rhonda said.

Aada nodded.

"Well, I promise not to force you to do anything you don't want to do."

Aada's body relaxed slightly.

Rhonda continued: "Going back to why you're here with me now, do you want to tell me a little bit about what happened with your last job?"

"They asked me to get *some help*"—Aada emphasized the last two words with air quotes—"and put me on forced medical leave, which they called a *sabbatical*. Probably to save their reputation. When I insisted that everything was fine, they fired me! They kept telling me I was behaving erratically and that I had too many absences that made me unfit to teach."

Rhonda sensed that there was more to the story. "I'm sorry to hear about that. And what about now? How are you feeling now?"

Aada squirmed in her seat. "I'm fine."

"There's no need to act tough in here, Aada. It sounds like you've had a rough go of things."

Aada looked Rhonda in the eye. Her gaze was intense and unflinching. "I feel like I've had an awful trick played on me. I lost my job, my girlfriend, I got evicted. From what I can tell, you can't trust anyone."

"That's a lot, Aada. I'm sorry. Do you have any friends or family you can reach out to?"

"No friends left. There's just my sister, but she's not speaking to me. We've never gotten along, but after our parents died things got so much worse. I tried to keep in touch for a while, but she never picked up my calls. I think there's just too much baggage there. Then my phone was stolen and whatever semblance of a relationship I had with her voicemail box just ended."

"How old is your sister?"

"She turned 23 a few months ago…" Aada cleared her throat. "But we're getting off topic. I'm here to get a job."

Rhonda needed more details, but she could sense that Aada was trying to avoid talking about her past. *Be patient,* she thought to herself. After all, Rhonda had only just met this woman and needed to create a rapport. "I can certainly help you find some work, Aada. We'll go through a database of available options you'd be qualified for and make some calls, but let's start with getting you back on your feet. What about some housing and maybe some clothes for interviews? We have food stamps available and even free bus passes. How does that sound?"

Aada began to well up.

It wasn't the first time a small gesture of care had induced tears in Rhonda's office. More than housing, food, or even a shower, most of her clients were overwhelmed when someone showed sincere care about their well-being. Rhonda leaned forward and tried to make eye contact with Aada. "Aada, I want you to know, even though I just met you, I care about you. You're not alone anymore. I'm here to help you and together we'll do what we can to get you back on your feet, okay?"

Aada crumpled, and through her sobs, she explained, "I worry so much. Not just about my career and my sister, but about things that I've never had to care about before. Like where am I going to pee? Why is peeing such a crime? Or would anyone notice if I died? I've never felt so alone." Aada stood up. She pulled off her trench coat and pointed at the faded tag. "Look. I used to shop at Prada. This is the only thing I have left from my past life. That and these shoes." She pulled off a dingy ballet flat with a broken bow and holes in the sides. "These are Steve Madden, but you can't tell anymore." She stuffed her foot back into her shoe and sat down. "I want my family back. I want my sister in my life again. I know I came in looking for a job, but more than anything I just want to be in a place where I feel like I belong, where someone knows me, like *really* knows me, and cares whether I live or die. Yeah, it sucks being looked through and I hate being so preoccupied with where I'm going to get food, but it's soul crushing knowing I don't matter to anyone."

Rhonda walked around the desk and gently placed her hand on Aada's shoulder.

Aada sniffled while she kept talking. "I can't think straight with this stupid headache. I'm tired and hungry and grimy and I just want to go home." Aada's eyes darted around, as if catching flickers of memory. There was an intensity to her gaze, like that of a wild tiger suddenly finding herself in a cage, desperate to be set free.

Rhonda knew this face. Every client she'd ever helped had something holding them back, some past trauma holding them hostage. It didn't matter if her clients had done horrible, violent things to others, or had self-medicated their emotional pain in destructive ways, at some point each of them shared the same look of vulnerability. It was this look that drove Rhonda. "Let's get you some help, Aada. That's what I'm here for. Please trust me when I say that I'll to do everything in my power to get you back on your feet." Rhonda returned to her chair on the other side of the desk.

"Thank you," Aada whispered. She pulled her shoulders back, wiped her eyes and continued: "You should know I'm not here for handouts. I know how to work hard. I'm not interested in charity."

"I believe you," said Rhonda. Chills went up and down her spine. As much as she tried to impact the lives of her clients, some clients had an even bigger impact on Rhonda. Engrossed in Aada's story, Rhonda had lost track of time. She still had a dozen questions she wanted to ask: *What was the timeline for all these events in Aada's life? Was there a moment that caused this unraveling, or was it gradual? What drugs was she asked to take? Anti- depressives or anti-psychotics or something else?* Rhonda focused again on Aada's sharing. *Don't get ahead of yourself, Rhonda.* "I'm so glad you came to see me, Aada. For someone who has been through so much, like yourself, it can feel nice to talk to someone about everything. We're lucky to have a few therapists on staff here and they're really lovely people. I can book you an appointment as early as this afternoon, if you like. What do you think?"

Aada stared blankly at Rhonda.

Rhonda wasn't sure what Aada's reaction meant, so she continued to explain: "They're all highly trained in psychotherapy, and I'd personally introduce you. Then we can check back in and get that paperwork rolling so we can find you some more stable housing and get you some food stamps. Does that sound good?"

Aada stood up abruptly. In a monotone voice she said, "I need to use the bathroom."

"Sure. Yes, of course. It's just down the hall to your right."

Aada headed out the door as Rhonda began collecting the necessary paperwork to get her sorted out with some services. Rhonda worked on auto pilot and allowed her mind to wander. She'd been embarrassed by her flippant reaction to Aada's story, and hoped it hadn't been too obvious. *A college professor? That woman? Then again,* she thought, *people living on the edge come in all shapes and sizes. You can't do this job well if you start off with all kinds of preconceived notions about who you're serving.* Everyone Rhonda had met experienced trauma, but it wasn't always like in the books or movies. It wasn't necessarily dramatic or wrought with external torture or agony. No, sometimes people just slowly careened off their path and were unsure how to regain their direction.

A sudden knock on the door pulled Rhonda out of her thoughts. A perky 20- something woman in jeans and a hoodie bearing the Evergreen Woman's Shelter logo poked her head into the office. "Rhonda? Your 2:30 is here."

Rhonda glanced at the clock. 2:40. "Oh, my gosh! Okay. Let me wrap things up with Aada."

"And what should I tell your next client?"

"Tell them I'll be right there." Rhonda skirted past the intern and headed to the woman's bathroom. She wanted to hurry things along with Aada so she could nail down a second appointment. It wasn't in Rhonda's nature to surprise clients on the toilet, but it was important to make sure Aada felt cared for.

At the entrance to the bathroom, Rhonda asked, "Aada? Are you in here?" No answer. Rhonda checked underneath the stalls. The room was empty. She stepped back into the hallway and looked around to see if Aada was making her way back to the office, but the hallway was quiet, save for a few interns checking their phones. Rhonda groaned and approached one of them. "Have you seen a tall woman, brown hair down to here, wearing a trench coat?"

The intern looked up from her phone in a daze, "Sorry, Rhonda. I was totally distracted. What did you just ask me?"

"Never mind." Rhonda headed to her office. She hoped against hope that Aada would be waiting inside. But her office was empty. Rhonda dialed the front desk to see if Aada had taken a wrong turn.

As the phone rang, the intern reappeared in the doorway. "Rhonda?"

'What?" Rhonda said. She sounded more exasperated than she meant to. "Sorry. It's just your 2:30, Jude, is still waiting?"

Rhonda slammed the phone receiver down and stood up. She poked her head into the hallway one more time to check for Aada. Rhonda returned to her desk and flopped into her chair. She'd have to move on. "All right, Casey. I'm ready."

The intern disappeared and Rhonda tried to collect her thoughts.

Rhonda reached into the mini fridge behind her and pulled out a bottle of water. She grabbed a granola bar from the basket on top and set them on the opposite side of her desk. A pot of coffee was still half full and warming in the back corner of her office, and there were plenty of paper cups and napkins at the ready. She pulled a thick file from the cabinet next to her and took a deep breath. *Smile, Rhonda.*

A woman with red curls, about 5'3" wearing a quilted button-up jacket, sweatpants and a beanie sauntered into her office. "Man," the woman said, "you had me waiting a long time, Ms. Rhonda."

"Hi, Jude. I'm so sorry about the wait. I must have lost track of time, but you're here now, and that's what matters."

Jude narrowed her eyes as she went about making herself at home in Rhonda's office. She moved with familiarity as she got herself a cup of coffee and grabbed for the granola bar on the desk. Jude slumped into the chair across from Rhonda, and got the appointment started. "So I got jumped last night, *again,* and there wasn't nobody around to see it. These two girls came at me and…"

5

If it were up to Elizabeth, attending college would be her full-time job. She was excited to graduate, but she'd miss campus life, not to mention she had zero direction for what to do afterward. Thinking too hard about it always made her anxious. Elizabeth adjusted her glasses and tried to refocus on labeling the 800 test tubes in front of her. Her smart watch buzzed, letting her know that her supervisor would arrive imminently. 3, 2, 1... The door swung open violently as a flushed, dripping-wet woman walked through.

"Hi, Luca. Right on time, I see!" Elizabeth teased.

"Give me a break, Liz."

Apparently it had not been a good morning for Luca. Elizabeth wasn't surprised. Luca often had mood swings that coincided with gloomy weather or talk of her older sister, Aada. Elizabeth had discovered that last trigger the hard way. Early on in her internship, Elizabeth had made the mistake of asking Luca if she was related to Professor Aada Talbot who taught at Beacon Hill Community College, since they shared the same last name. Elizabeth knew it was a far shot, but she had to ask because Ms. Talbot had been Elizabeth's all-time favorite professor. It turned out they were sisters, but not the bosom-buddy kind. More like the Amy and Jo March from *Little Women* kind.

It seemed like it should have been a fairytale: two sisters in the sciences of all things! One taught philosophy, and the other was a highly respected microbiologist doctoral candidate. Elizabeth was an only child and had often fantasized about having a brother or sister. But after seeing Luca's reaction at the mere mention of Ms. Talbot, Elizabeth had wondered if she'd been spared some heartache. After all, there was no guarantee that, had she had a sibling, they would have liked each other at all. She didn't know why Ms. Talbot and Luca were on such bad terms, but she knew not to bring it up.

Luca dumped her messenger bag in the corner of the lab and draped her jacket on the back of a stool. She donned her lab coat and squelched over in her wet shoes to where Elizabeth was standing.

"Your umbrella didn't join you today, huh?" Elizabeth joked.

"Something like that." Luca examined one of the test tubes Elizabeth had labeled. "These look good. Go ahead and start working on those 10 ml ones over there. I need 500 of them. I'll be back."

"Okay…" Elizabeth was accustomed to Luca arriving late. But where could she possibly need to go after having just arrived?

Luca sighed and pointed at her soggy curls. "I'm going to stick my head under the blow dryer in the bathroom and think about my life choices. Is that okay with you?" Luca stormed out through the double doors.

Well, Elizabeth thought, *she's been in worse moods!*

Elizabeth returned to labeling test tubes and fretting about her graduation ceremony. Everything was set except for one detail. She wanted Ms. Talbot to be there. For the past two years, Elizabeth had enrolled in every philosophy class Ms. Talbot had taught. Then her favorite professor and advisor went on sabbatical without telling any of her students. Elizabeth had emailed but never got a response. To be honest, she was left feeling confused and a bit hurt. Elizabeth had thought she had a strong connection with Ms. Talbot and took her silence personally. Elizabeth hadn't thought about what to do if Ms. Talbot didn't return in time for graduation, and now she was against a deadline. The department chair needed the name of a professor who could do her graduation introduction by this Friday!

Another alarm from Elizabeth's smart watch made her jump. "Water break," it flashed. As she reached for her water bottle, she couldn't help but look at the calendar on the wall. The red X's across each day seemed like a cruel reminder of her looming deadline. Monday - X, Tuesday - X, Wednesday - well, that was today.

Elizabeth bit her lower lip. *Don't do it!* She told herself.

Luca came back into the lab.

"All better?" Elizabeth asked.

"At least I won't drip on the lab equipment anymore. That's something."

Elizabeth laughed half-heartedly and returned to her colorful tapes. They worked together in silence for a long time. All the while, Elizabeth silently mulled over her dilemma. Three hours into the work day, Elizabeth couldn't ignore the facts any longer. She had one option for getting in touch with Ms. Talbot, and if she didn't take it, she may miss her chance forever. It would just take a lot of courage, or stupidity. Elizabeth wasn't sure which. "So, Luca," Elizabeth started. "I've been meaning to ask you something."

"Uh-huh. So ask me," Luca said.

"You know I respect you and your work and I think you're great, right?"

"What are you getting at?" Luca turned to face Elizabeth.

"I know you told me not to bring her up again—"

"Oh, God."

"Hear me out."

"You're talking about Aada, aren't you?"

Elizabeth paused. "Here's the thing—"

"Nope. Not interested."

"Come on. Please?" Elizabeth jumped in front of Luca, who had made it a habit of becoming intensely interested in staplers or ball point pens at any mention of Aada.

Luca turned around and headed toward the back counter. "I've told you before. Not. Interested!"

Elizabeth looked at the calendar and took a deep breath. *If there were ever a time to poke the bear, this would be it.* Then she let all the words tumble out of her as fast as she could in hopes of getting it out before Luca could cut her off again. "Your sister has been on sabbatical for almost a year and she's not returning any of my emails. The department secretary won't give me any details because of confidentiality policies and I just want to see if she's willing to show up for my graduation ceremony as my advisor, and I have to let the department know she's my advisor by Friday, and it's already Wednesday, and I don't have any backup advisor, and I don't really want a backup advisor because I just really want her to be there." Elizabeth held her breath as she stared at the back of Luca's head. More silence. Elizabeth continued in a whisper: "I need her confirmation by Friday."

Luca turned her head and checked the wall calendar. "Sort of waited till the last minute, huh."

Elizabeth let out her breath. *At least Luca's talking.* "Yeah. Kind of."

Luca went back to filling trays with rows of brightly labeled test tubes. "Look, Elizabeth, I haven't heard from Aada since October. I don't think I'll be much help."

Elizabeth blinked. "Oh. I didn't realize. I know you two aren't on great terms, but I didn't realize you were completely—"

"Well, now you know."

Elizabeth was crestfallen. *Now what am I going to do? Luca hasn't heard from her sister in months and I've just made the next few hours incredibly uncomfortable for myself all for naught.* Trying to refocus, Elizabeth kept worrying. *It just doesn't add up. Why would Ms. Talbot leave me so suddenly? At the very least, wouldn't she stay in touch with her sister? What could Luca have done that was so horrible? Or maybe Ms. Talbot did something? No. She's amazing! Luca's squandering an incredible opport—*

"She's on sabbatical, huh?" Luca said.

"Oh. I guess so. That's what the department secretary said. But it's strange. Your sister never told us anything, and she left mid-way through a quarter after she had already been sick for a while. Don't you think she would have at least finished the term?"

"I don't try to guess what Aada thinks. It's easier for me to just ignore her."

"Sure. I guess that makes sense." Elizabeth went back to ripping bits of colored tape off the spool and Luca went back to the centrifuge. "I'm sorry." Elizabeth said.

Luca narrowed her eyes.

Elizabeth continued: "For bringing her up, for how your relationship is, for myself, and not having a mentor anymore. I'm just sorry."

Luca said nothing.

The air was thick with disappointment. Elizabeth went back to her test tubes. Their cheerful stripes seemed to mock her as they lay together in the tray. She tried to hold back her tears, but a sniffle got through.

Luca groaned and came over to the table where Elizabeth stood. "Look. Aada and I don't have a great relationship, but that's not your fault. You didn't sell my childhood home out from under me, and you didn't abandon me when our parents died, so I guess it's not really fair for me to take out my anger with Aada on you." Luca paused. "I'm sorry too."

Now it was Elizabeth's turn to look shocked. "I didn't know."

"Failed families aren't a topic that come up very often with causal work colleagues." Luca flashed a toothy grin.

Elizabeth appreciated her supervisor's attempt at humor and smiled back. "No. I guess not."

"But hey, she didn't ruin your life, so here." Luca scribbled something onto a sticky note and stuck it to the center of the table.

Elizabeth's eyes widened. "Is that…?" She gingerly peeled the sticky note off the table and stared at what could only be a phone number.

"Like I said, I haven't heard from her in months, but this was the last number she had."

Elizabeth felt giddy with anticipation. She wanted to give Luca a hug, but her supervisor had already moved on. Elizabeth closed her eyes and imagined the sparkling conversations she would have with Ms. Talbot. "Thank you so much, Luca! Really. You have no idea what this means to me."

Luca smiled. "Well, that's something, I guess."

Elizabeth carefully folded the sticky note and placed it in her lab coat pocket. She went back to work with a bounce in her step and a new outlook on life. Everything was falling into place.

Elizabeth was distracted as she boarded the bus to downtown. It had been two weeks since graduation and she was meeting with friends one last time before everyone went their separate ways. Her graduation ceremony hadn't gone as she had hoped, and she was still feeling rather blue. She never did get hold of Ms. Talbot, so the head of the department had introduced Elizabeth. It was painfully impersonal next to all the other graduates and their advisors. Elizabeth cringed at the memory of it as she found a window seat in the middle of the bus.

Elizabeth dialed Ms. Talbot's number without thinking and hoped this would be the time she answered. Graduation may have passed, but she still wanted to touch base with her advisor, if for no other reason than to clear the air around her sudden sabbatical and unanswered emails and phone calls.

There were no rings, just a robotic woman's voice saying the same thing it had a dozen times prior: "The person at this number has not set up their voicemail box. Good bye."

Elizabeth stuffed her phone back into her clutch and rested her head against the glass widow. The thumping of her temple against the glass was giving her a headache. She balled up her shrug cardigan to form a reasonable travel pillow. As she fidgeted around, a woman outside the window caught her attention.

The woman was shouting at an invisible aggressor, passionately gesticulated with one hand while the other hand held her head. She wore a long grey trench coat—or was it beige? Elizabeth wasn't sure. Bits of jacket were torn and sagging under the arms and the woman's hair was wild and matted on the top of her head. Something about the woman kept Elizabeth craning her neck to get a better look. The woman was tall and Elizabeth could tell she used to be quite stylish, what with her tattered dress shoes. The woman was only a distant silhouette beneath the street lamps when Elizabeth realized who it was.

"Ms. Talbot?!" Elizabeth yelled.

The old woman sharing the seat with Elizabeth jumped and said, "No, I'm not Ms. Talbot."

"Sorry, I didn't mean you." Elizabeth reached up and pulled the bell cord. Her heart was racing. She scooted past the woman in the aisle seat and made her way to the back door. The bus slowed to a stop after a few blocks and Elizabeth slipped out the back. She raced up the street.

In the dim light, Elizabeth wondered if she had seen things. *Am I delirious? Maybe I'm just tired from graduation.* She reached the spot she'd last seen the woman and her shoulders slumped. Whoever it had been, they were gone now. Elizabeth checked her watch. She had 20 minutes till the next bus.

Elizabeth wandered up and down the streets a few blocks in every direction. She was desperate to find the woman. But all she could picture was Ms. Talbot as she had remembered her: tall, slender, modern but classic, confident to a fault. Elizabeth couldn't help herself. She sat down on the curb next to the bust stop and allowed herself to cry for the first time since everything had unraveled.

6

"Get off me!" the patient screamed at Sara, the ER nurse.

The CT technician stood like a deer in headlights as she watched Sara wrangle the patient into the machine.

"There's no way you're getting me into that thing!" the patient screamed as she pulled out of Sara's grip and scrambled to the other side of the room.

"Aada, there's nothing to be afraid of," Sara barked. "If you just lie down in the machine, we can take a picture of your brain and see what's causing your headaches. It's perfectly safe. You've got to trust me."

The patient glared at Sara.

Sara exchanged knowing glances with the CT tech as they each moved in on the patient from opposite sides. This wasn't their first rodeo together.

"No way! Not like this! I'm not getting in there, and you're not pumping me up with whatever drugs you've got in that bag!" the patient protested.

Sara spoke to the patient as she and the CT tech circled around her. "Aada, right now we don't have enough information to treat you. Beyond prescribing pain medication to address your symptoms, we can't tell why your headaches keep recurring. But this machine—"

The patient stopped dead in her tracks and faced Sara. "I'm not going in there! Give me back my clothes!"

Sara was sick of playing games. "Look," she said, "I don't have a lot of time. There's a waiting room full of patients out there that aren't going anywhere until I see them, so get in that machine right now! Don't you understand we're tying to help you?!" It was 2 a.m. and the last thing Sara wanted to deal with was a hysterical patient.

The patient slowly backed away from Sara until she was pressed up against the wall of the exam room. Then her whole body slumped down onto the linoleum floor and she began to cry. Sara looked at her watch and huffed. "Okay, Aada. I'm going to give you some space. I'll be back in a moment with some water." Sara signaled to the CT tech to keep an eye on the patient as she left the room. Outside in the hallway, she leaned against the wall and rested her head in her hands. *What are you going to do now, Sara?* she thought to herself. This wasn't how she envisioned a career in nursing.

Suddenly the exam door cracked opened and the technician popped her head into the hallway.

Sara straightened up. "Everything okay?"

"She's just lying there. Still crying."

Sara took a deep breath and closed her eyes.

"I was thinking," the tech continued, "didn't someone come in with her? Maybe you could bring her back here to help her calm down?"

"Brilliant! Why didn't I think of that? I'll go get her." Sara headed down the corridor toward the waiting room.

The woman who had come in with Sara's patient was sitting in a blue vinyl chair, her legs draped over another chair as she watched TV. She wore a plaid quilted jacket and sweat pants. Her matted red hair fell down to her shoulders in clumps.

Sara cleared her throat. "Excuse me, ma'am. Did you come in with Aada?"

The woman tumbled out of the chair and stood in front of Sara. "Is everything all right?"

"We're having some difficulty persuading your friend to get a CT scan, and we hoped you might be able to help."

The woman screwed up her face. "What do you want me to do?"

"Can you come and talk to her? We really can't do much for her without that scan."

"Okay. I'll see what I can do. But you know you're the doctor, right?" The woman winked at Sara and smiled.

Sara's shoulders relaxed and she smiled back. "What's your name?"

"Jude."

"Nice to meet you. You can call me Nurse Sara."

"Pleased to meet you, Nurse Sara."

"While we're walking, can you tell me anything else about your friend? Did she have a bad experience in a hospital or something?"

"Well, from what I've been able to figure out, she don't like doctors too much. Doesn't trust them. She's got a bit of a history with them telling her what to do and what to take. She hasn't given me much of the details, but I think she sort of went crazy or something and had to be hospitalized. Or maybe they wanted her to be hospitalized but she wouldn't go. I'm not really sure of the details. She doesn't particularly like talking about it."

Sara tried to choose her words carefully. "She seems pretty reluctant."

"Hah! That's an understatement! I practically had to drag her ass here. But when she kept talking funny and falling over dizzy, I was pretty sure it was more than just a headache. Plus, she wouldn't even take Tylenol. 'It's a drug,' she'd say, 'and I don't take drugs!'" Jude rolled her eyes in amusement.

Sara and Jude continued their walk in silence. They passed a drinking fountain and Sara paused to fill a cup with water. When they arrived at the door to the CT room, Sara turned to Jude and said, "You're a good friend. Let's hope you can get through to her."

They entered the room. The tech was keeping an eye on the patient from behind a computer monitor on the desk in the corner of the room. The patient had moved closer to the door, but was still in a heap on the floor, sobbing quietly.

Sara saw Jude's face drop. *Maybe this was a mistake,* Sara thought.

"Hey, Aada," Jude crooned. "It's me, Jude." There was no response. "What are you doing on the floor?" Jude slowly made her way over to Aada and knelt down beside her.

Sara passed a cup of water to Jude. "Here's some water if she wants," she whispered.

Jude reached to take the cup, never taking her eyes off her friend. "You know, these doctors are good doctors. They want to help you so badly. Me too. We all want you to feel better." Jude tried to make eye contact with Aada. "Want some water?"

The patient looked up and gingerly took the cup. She drank greedily, never breaking eye contact with Jude.

"Hey. There she is. Hi, Aada. It's me, Jude." Jude smiled at her friend. "What do you say we give these doctors a chance to help you out?"

The patient shook her head violently and spoke in a hushed tone: "They just want to pump me full of drugs and tell me I'm crazy."

Jude raised an eyebrow. "I don't think that's what's going on, Aada. They're just trying to figure out how to fix your headaches and your dizziness and your blurry eyes and your throwing up."

"You don't understand! This is what happened last time!"

"Wait, you mean at the college?" Jude asked.

The patient turned to stare Sara straight in the eye. "They say they want to help, but really they're trying to do experiments on me!"

At this, Sara jumped in. "Aada, I promise you we're not trying to do any experiments on you. Nobody is. But we are trying to help you out and even your friend Jude wants you to do the scan. She's worried about you and wants you to get better. Don't you want to feel better?"

The patient stared at Jude and spoke through clenched teeth: "I don't want to do this."

"But we can't just leave. You need help." Jude said.

"No, I don't! Honestly, I don't know why we're friends!"

At that, Jude was up on her feet, arms flailing in the air. "Well, fine then! Excuse me for bringing you here! Serves me right for giving a damn about you! Do whatever the hell you want, Aada!"

"Whoah, whoah, whoah. Hold on," Sara said, trying to get a hold of the situation.

Jude knocked into Sara as she stormed toward the door.

Sara shot a knowing look at the tech and headed out the door after Jude. "Jude! Wait up!" Sara caught up with the woman in time to see her wipe away a few tears.

"Aada just goes crazy sometimes!" Jude shouted as she walked at break-neck speed down the corridor. "She hates it when I point it out, but sometimes she's just not right in the head! I don't know what to do when she's like this! Usually I just let her sleep it off, or something! But now we're here and I can't do that!"

Sara tried to keep up, but she was quickly out of breath. "You're really nice to stick it out with your friend," she called out. "She's lucky to have you." Sara stopped and put her hands on her knees. She was way out of shape.

Jude slowed down and turned to face Sara. "I hate to admit it, but she's all I've got." Jude waited for Sara to walk to where she stood. "To be honest, I'm all she's got, too. Sucks caring about people."

Sara put a hand on Jude's shoulder; the other hand massaged a stitch in her side. As impatient as she was, Sara's heart was softening. Watching the dynamic between these two women had opened her up. "She means a lot to you, doesn't she?"

Jude let out a heavy sob as Sara pulled her in for a hug. "We can't change people," Sara continued. "We can only meet them where they're at."

They stood like that for several minutes.

Jude eventually pulled away from Sara and Sara saw the worried look in Jude's eyes. "Let's give it one more try," Sara said. "You never know. Maybe the tech did some magic while we were gone. And if Aada doesn't go for it, well, we're just going to have to be okay with that. It's still really good you brought her in."

Jude wiped her nose and eyes with the sleeve of her jacket. "Yeah, okay."

Sara mouthed a little prayer under her breath as they headed back down the corridor to the CT room in silence. *These two women need each other. Please, let me do what I can to help.*

7

Emmy stepped through the doorway of the house she shared with her wife of twenty years. She laid her briefcase on the back of the couch and kicked off her shoes. The French doors leading to the back yard were wide open and everything in their open-concept home was touched by sunlight. There was an abandoned cup of tea and an open book on the fireplace mantle, but where was Jamie?

"Jamie, I'm home," Emmy called out.

She heard her wife's distant voice coming from the back yard: "I'm out here. Come join us."

Us? Emmy thought to herself. "Do we have company? Should I put my clothes back on?" Emmy joked.

"WHAT!? What are you talking about?"

"Just kidding. I'll be right there." Emmy slipped on her house shoes and made her way across the living room and into the dining room where the French doors stood wide open, an energy suck even when they were closed. Still, they were beautiful and served as a window to their stunning yard. Jamie was a landscape designer and the yard was an extension of their perfectly curated house.

Emmy stood at the top of the porch and took a deep breath. The air was cool and refreshing. She cupped her eyes and scanned the yard for her wife. The sun was still high in the sky, even though it was 6 p.m. "Where are you?"

"Over here." Jamie waved to Emmy. She was sitting on a stone bench near a small koi pond. The leaves of the Japanese maple above her were a brilliant green and offered some much appreciated shade. The yard was beautiful any time of the year, but served as a second living room during the summer months. Beside Jamie sat Luca, looking flustered and upset. Emmy's stomach lurched. She forced a smile as she made her way down the porch steps. "Luca. What are you doing here?"

Luca was Emmy's god-daughter. Her mother, Lily, had been like a sister to Emmy. After Lily and her husband died, Emmy tried to stay in touch with the girls, but everyone went their separate ways to grieve. Still, Emmy regretted how things had unfolded. Aada had requested Emmy to sell the family home only a few months after Lily's passing, but Luca wasn't ready. Emmy could still hear the girls shouting at each other the day Luca found out. Tears had poured down all their faces as Luca stormed off, shouting, "Traitors! I'm never talking to any of you again!" Emmy wasn't sure if she was glad to see Luca, or still upset by all that had transpired. For Luca to cut Emmy out of her life was a loss that still stung.

Emmy made her way across the yard and did her best to sound unfazed. "Hi. It's been a while."

Jamie looked at Emmy and screwed up her face as if to say, *Really? That's the best you can do?*

"Yeah, I know. I'm sorry to stop by like this. I know we didn't end on the best of terms, but you're the only people I know from, you know. You're the closest thing I've got to family."

"Okay?" Emmy moved Luca's bag onto the ground and sat down beside her.

"I think Aada's in trouble," Luca said.

"What sort of trouble, hon?" Jamie asked.

"She's missing."

"How would you know?" Emmy asked, sounding more judgmental than she meant.

"Well, you remember that day in front of our old house?"

Emmy felt her stomach drop. "Yeah. I remember."

"Aada called me every Wednesday after that and left me a message, but about nine months ago, her messages stopped. At first I thought she had just given up on me, but now I think something's really wrong."

Emmy's heart felt heavy. She knew more about those phone calls than Luca realized, because after every phone call Luca ignored, Emmy got a call from Aada in tears. *If only Luca knew how hurt her sister was by all those missed opportunities.* "Get to the point, Luca."

Luca looked surprised by Emmy's harsh tone, but continued: "Aada makes me crazy and there are times when I just see red when I think about her, but deep down, I think she cared about me in her own screwed-up way. I just never really saw it for what it was. She's so difficult to get along with, but I still want to know that she's all right. We're sisters."

Emmy sighed. She understood that grief could do strange things with people's emotions. "Your sister does care about you, Luca, very much." Emmy paused to let that sink in. "But did it ever occur to you that your sister may have stuff going on of her own?"

"I suppose that's probably true. After she left for undergrad our relationship got so much worse. Even when she was home for those six months to do some sort of research project, she'd lock her self up in that attic bedroom. I never knew what was going on with her, or if she even came down to eat. I may have been an annoying middle school kid, but if she had stuff going on, she could have talked to me about it instead of shutting me out."

Jamie cleared her throat. "I think we're getting a little off track. Luca, sweetie, what Emmy is trying to say is, what are you doing here *now*? Why, after more than a year of silence, are you sitting here in our backyard wondering where Aada is?"

Luca stood up and faced both women. "There's this intern, Elizabeth, who worked for me last semester. She took all of Aada's classes at Beacon Hill and ogled her like she was some sort of rock star. She wanted to get in touch with Aada before her graduation in June, and asked for her number. Apparently Aada wasn't responding to email. Then, a few weeks after graduation, Elizabeth called me out of the blue and said she thought she saw Aada on the street near our building."

"In front of your lab?" Emmy asked.

"Yeah."

"That's downtown, where people often walk around."

"Yeah?"

Emmy paused. "And that's significant because…?"

Luca sighed. "You don't understand. Elizabeth said she saw Aada *on the street*—like she was living there. Like she was homeless."

There was a desperate look in Luca's eyes. "Slow down," Jamie said. "Aada's an adjunct professor at a community college. What makes you or your intern think she could be homeless?"

"According to Elizabeth, Aada was on sabbatical, and the department secretary wouldn't give her any details about when she was coming back or how to get in touch with her. She tried Aada's work email but never heard anything."

"Maybe Aada's somewhere really remote and doesn't have access to email or cell reception," Jamie suggested.

Emmy quietly pulled out her phone and scrolled through her call history. *Had it really been six months since Aada had called?* Emmy felt a wave of guilt wash over her and she shot a concerned look in Jamie's direction.

"What?" Luca said. Her gaze bounced back and forth between the two women's faces. "Do you know something?"

Emmy tried to sound as unconcerned as possible: "I haven't spoken to Aada for a while, but I bet she's fine.

Jamie's right. If she's on sabbatical, she could be anywhere in the world."

"No. I saw that look you gave Jamie. What are you trying to cover up?"

"Why don't you come sit back down," Emmy said.

"No. I'm fine, thank you. Now tell me what's going on." Luca crossed her arms as she stood.

"I'm sure your sister's fine," Jamie repeated as she looked sideways at Emmy.

"Tell me what's going on!"

Jamie sighed. "Do you remember when you were in middle school and your mom was always so eager to get you into different clubs and after-school activities?"

"Go on," Luca said.

"Well, while you were at your music lessons and dance classes, your mom would often be dealing with your sister. They'd go to therapy so she could learn strategies to help her keep organized, regulate her emotions, and rein in her day-dreaming."

"So what? She had ADD or something?"

Emmy picked up the story at this point. "That was the original diagnosis, and for a while it seemed like it was pretty accurate. Aada was doing really well with the strategies the doctor had taught her, and your parents sort of let your sister do her thing. Then she enrolled in college. The cognitive load was just too much and during her sophomore year, her strategies stopped being effective. Her imagination took over and she started having scary hallucinations and hearing voices. She got really paranoid. Your mom picked her up from college and brought her home. They told you she was doing research, but that wasn't altogether honest."

Luca stared blankly at Emmy.

Emmy continued: "When Aada came home during her undergrad years to do what your mom called 'research projects' she went back to her old therapist. Eventually, they figured out that she had schizoaffective bipolar disorder, not ADD, and switched her to a psychiatrist close to the university. Knowing Aada's true condition, your parents and the doctors were able to get her on the right meds and give her coping strategies that were really effective. She was so high functioning that she went back to university and thrived."

"But we could also see," Jamie cautiously noted, "how the stress of losing your parents so suddenly could have agitated her condition."

"And without the support of your parents," Emmy added, "what with your mom and dad being so involved in the management of her condition, she may not have been able to recover on her own." Emmy let the weight of her words settle and watched Luca's face for any reaction.

Luca stared off into the distance, past Jamie and Emmy. Dusk had arrived and the maple leaves beside them became nearly black in the dim light. Solar-powered lanterns flickered on around them.

"Luca? Sweetie? Are you okay?" Jamie asked.

Luca said nothing for a long time. Then, in a hushed voice, she replied, "Why wasn't I told about any of this?"

"It's not something your parents liked talking about, and Aada really struggled with accepting her diagnosis," Jamie clarified.

"It wasn't a secret per se, but it also wasn't a topic any of them enjoyed talking about. You know your parents. I loved them, but they really believed that if they didn't talk about it, it would just go away," said Emmy.

"Besides, you and Aada lived pretty separate lives, even under the same roof. When things got difficult for Aada during college, they didn't see a point in involving you," said Jamie.

Luca narrowed her eyes. She balled her hands into fists and spoke through clenched teeth. "Do you realize how different things could have been had I known about this?"

Emmy stared at Luca in bewilderment. *How is this my fault?* she thought to herself.

"I could have had an actual relationship with Aada! Instead of walking out on her after our parents died, we could have comforted each other. Maybe I could have even helped her! Don't you see? Not knowing about this may have cost me any hope of being a family!"

Emmy was overwhelmed. She was hurt that Luca was blaming her. The conversation was opening old wounds that still hadn't healed. She missed her friend Lily and felt guilty for not digging deeper into the distance between Luca and Aada. Emmy chastised herself for getting so distracted with her own life and not noticing when Aada's phone calls stopped. Tears welled up in her eyes, and her voice cracked as she spoke. "I'm sorry, Luca. Maybe you're right. Maybe knowing this stuff would have made a difference, but I also think your parents never wanted you to feel responsible for Aada. They knew this would be a life-long struggle and I think they were just trying to protect you."

"And what about you? Were you trying to protect me from having any scraps of my family left once my parents were gone?!"

"It wasn't our news to share!" Emmy was up on her feet. Anger, guilt, fear and worry darted through her mind like balls in a pinball machine. "We thought about trying to convince Aada to tell you, but even you have to acknowledge that things kind of fell apart when the house went up for sale and you walked out on all of us!"

"Babe. Honey. Emmy." Jamie crooned. "Take a breath. Why don't we all sit back down."

Emmy sat down slowly as Jamie turned to Luca. "Luca, you're here now," Jamie said, "and we'd really love for you to be part of our lives again. We've missed you. What we're telling you is everything we know, honest, and I'm sorry it's coming to you so late in the game."

Luca kept her gaze fixated on Jamie.

Emmy exhaled audibly as she mumbled, "You're not the only one who lost someone that day." She regretted it the moment the words left her lips.

Luca turned and glared at Emmy with tears streaming down her cheeks. "Don't you dare. You've no idea what I've been going through. I've filled out a missing person report, scanned the unclaimed remains police sketches, made eye contact with every homeless woman I've passed, and now I come to find out that all this could have been avoided if you'd just taken the time to fill me in on my own family history! For all I know, Aada's in some shelter, or worse, lying in a ditch, dead!" Luca grabbed her bag off the ground and stormed toward the gate.

Emmy's entire body slumped like a deflated balloon as she let her head fall forward into her hands. The tears came quickly and she didn't see a point in trying to stop them.

Jamie tried to catch up with Luca, but she was already unlatching the gate. "Luca, stop! Where are you going?"

"To find my sister!"

8

Bzzz, bzzz, bzzz. "Where is it?!" Eileen cried. Stacks of papers and books crashed to the floor as she searched through the piles on her desk. *Bzzz, bzzz, bzzz.* "Damnit! As if this office isn't small enough. Now it eats phones?!" Eileen was an adjunct professor at Beacon Hill Community College and had little more than a closet to call her own. Still, she wouldn't give up her office for anything. Cozy spaces suited her. Now if she could just channel her inner Marie Kondo and organize everything!

Bzzz, bzzz. bzzz. "Oh, come on!" Then silence. Eileen fell into her chair. There on her desk, peeking out from beneath a pile of essays from her Philosophy 101 course, sat her phone. Eileen scowled at the lifeless piece of plastic and snatched it out from under the papers. A long-forgotten name flashed across her screen. *Luca? What's she doing calling me?* The phone vibrated to indicate there was a voicemail message. *I'll check it later,* Eileen said to herself and plopped the phone on top of her messy desk. Whatever new drama was about to unfold, it could wait. But then a text appeared: "Eileen. It's Luca. Can we talk?"

Eileen's stomach dropped. She had spent the last six months trying to forget about Aada. Recovering from their breakup was taking longer than she wanted. But it made sense considering they'd planned to spend the rest of their lives together.

Guilt washed over Eileen. She still cared for Aada, and had intended to check in on her once the dust of their breakup had settled. Her memories brought up mixed feelings. Sometimes they left her with a smile, but more often then not they catapulted her into days of numbness. The trauma was still too real. Their relationship had been full of passion and laughter, but also stress and hostility. Love hadn't been enough to keep them together. Eileen's therapist, Dr. Anderson, kept encouraging her to allow the process to unfold at its own pace, but Eileen was tired of processing. She wanted to be through to the other side already.

Eileen picked up her phone and typed: "Luca, it's been a while..." *No, too informal*, she thought, and deleted her message. "Hi, Luca. I'm not sure..." Eileen put the phone down and rubbed her eyes. Straight ahead of her was a wall calendar with an image of a lush forest. It was the closest thing she had to a window. The image reminded her of the house she and Aada had dreamed of building. Their backyard was going to open up to a huge garden and then wilderness as far as the eye could see. And then there were the children—two boys and a girl—who would play in the yard with their free-range chickens. She smiled at the memory of her and Aada, curled up on the couch, planning their future together. But Eileen's face drooped as the more traumatic memories of their relationship invaded her daydream.

Eileen tried composing the message again: "Hello, Luca. It's been a while. Can you tell me what you want to talk about?" *Maybe Luca wanted career advice? Maybe it's not about Aada at all.*

The phone buzzed in Eileen's hand. She read Luca's text: "Eileen, I can't get a hold of Aada. She won't answer my texts and my calls go straight to voicemail. I know you don't like getting in the middle of our relationship, but what's going on with her?"

Eileen sighed. *Luca must not know we broke up, not that it's any of her business.* Eileen looked up at the ceiling and debated just how involved she wanted to get with her ex's little sister. "I'm sorry to hear she's not responding, but I'm afraid I can't help you." Eileen paused. "We're not together anymore. My advice is to give her some time." Eileen hit send.

An uneasy feeling bubbled up in Eileen's stomach. This wasn't the first time Aada had disappeared. A few months after Aada's parents died, she disappeared for three days. They'd both left for work that morning, but only Eileen came home in the evening. She called everyone they knew. After 24 hours Eileen filed a missing person report with the city police. Two days later, Aada turned up at home. Her hair and clothes were disheveled and her face was criss-crossed with lines as if she'd aged a decade. Eileen had stood at the doorway and watched Aada crawl to their front door, occasionally hiding behind bushes on her way. She had a wild look in her eyes and when she got inside, she couldn't stop talking about surveillance cameras and drones, medical tests and the people she'd escaped from.

The phone buzzed again. Another message from Luca: "I'm not playing around. I think she's missing."

"Damn it." Eileen tried to hold back her tears. *How could one text message dredge up so much?* A rush of emotions flooded her body as she replayed the two years she and Aada were together. Eileen was sick to her stomach. She could feel herself spiraling toward a whirlpool of bad memories and guilt. In a panic, she reached for her grandma's Swingline stapler and tried to focus on the cold metal in her hands. *You're not her girlfriend anymore, Eileen. Maintain your boundaries.* "Right," she said to her empty office.

Eileen set to work solving the problem of Luca. "I'm not sure what to say, but if you want to talk, my last class gets out at 4 p.m. tomorrow. We could meet on campus at the coffee shop in the student union building for an hour." Eileen hit send and took a deep breath.

"Thank you, Eileen. See you then," Luca replied immediately.

Eileen tossed the phone onto the desk and massaged her temples. She worked hard not to reminisce about her time with Aada. The only exception was during her weekly therapy appointments, but being confronted by her ex's little sister forced Eileen to delve into the past.

It had all started so innocently. They were both new to the college's philosophy department. Standing at the photocopier one day, Aada had made a quip about Descartes. Eileen had laughed. And that's all it took. They were inseparable after that. Passionate conversations about ethics, philosophy and sex led to dating and then living together, and for a while it was really great. Sure, it wasn't perfect, but what relationship was? Aada had a tendency to get paranoid from time to time, like when she thought the mailman was stalking her, and she had a difficult relationship with Luca, which she belabored ad nauseam, but a bit of paranoia and a strained family relationship were practically cliche. Nothing seemed particularly out of the ordinary.

It wasn't until they'd been living together for about a year that things unraveled. Aada's parents died in February and Aada couldn't cope. She'd held it together long enough to finalize her parents' estate and sell the house, but by that summer her quirky paranoia had intensified and she became suspicious of everything. The only way she seemed to find any relief was when she could successfully control her environment and Eileen. That meant staying at home as much as possible and going through endless rituals to make sure their food was untainted and that their house was debugged.

That fall, Eileen started going to work alone. When asked about Aada, she'd keep it brief: "She's not feeling well." *Technically I'm not lying,* she'd tell herself. Every few days, Eileen would come home to another boarded-up window or a new padlock on the front door. On occasion, Aada would tell Eileen that the drones were sleeping, and they were both able to go to work for a few weeks. But eventually the drones were replaced by a different conspiracy and her months of spotty attendance at work became several weeks of absences strung together. In Aada's world, everyone was plotting against her—from the dean of the school all the way down to the neighborhood dog walker. The college put Aada on sabbatical to give her time to recover—of what they were still unsure. But time ran out and Aada was unwilling to get help. By the end of fall term, Aada was asked to leave.

Eileen recalled the moment she handed Aada her termination letter. "So you're on their side?!" Aada had screamed.

"You haven't shown up for work in ages. They're worried about you! They did what they could to buy you the time you needed, but after your sabbatical was up they still needed someone to teach your classes. I really do think they want the best for you, and they even said they'd gladly reconsider hiring you once you got some help."

"Help? What do they mean by 'help'? I don't need help! What did you say to them? What if they're working with the drone people and now they know where I am!?" Aada's eyes had been wild and otherworldly. Eileen remembered how Aada had shoved her out of the way, running around the house to double-check that all her locks were in place. Eileen had lost her balance and fallen against the coffee table. Eileen rubbed her shoulder at the memory.

Eileen had done everything she could for Aada, but she was foolish to think their relationship would be enough. She'd considered walking away many times, but a few weeks after Aada had been put on sabbatical, she'd had a moment of lucidity and agreed to see a therapist. It didn't take long for the therapist to diagnose Aada with schizoaffective bipolar disorder. Eileen remembered how her stomach dropped as she heard this for the first time, but the therapist reassured her that it was possible to live a fulfilling life with therapy and medication. The mere mention of medication had sent Aada into a rage. "Are you freaking kidding me?! Not again! I'm not taking your drugs and I don't need your help. I'm sick of being gaslighted! And stop doing your experiments on me!" she shrieked. "I knew I never should have come. There's nothing wrong with me—not then, not now, not ever!" Eileen shuddered at the memory. She could still feel the floor vibrate as Aada walked out of the therapist's office and slammed the door so hard that the vase on the bookshelf crashed to the floor.

Eileen willed herself to return to the present. *I'm not there anymore. I'm in my office and I'm perfectly safe.* She couldn't help but remember the last words the therapist had said before she chased after Aada: "Eileen, Aada alluded to the possibility that she has some history with this diagnosis. Do you recall anything she's told you about her mental health in the past?"

"Nothing. She's not a fan of talking about the past."

"Hmmm. Well, there may be something there. If you can catch her in a lucid moment, you may want to probe her a bit about it. It might offer us insights into what treatments worked best for her in the past."

"I understand, but I have to be honest: I don't think there's much hope for me getting through to her."

"Well, I'll be straight with you. I can't do anything for Aada if she refuses treatment, but without treatment, a fulfilling life will be very difficult to secure. Talk to her. See if you can help her see that it's in her best interest to continue treatment. If she wants to continue with just therapy for now, we can certainly start there."

"Thank you. I'll talk to her." Eileen remembered the feeling of hopelessness as she stood up to leave the office.

"Eileen?" the therapist had called after her. "I know it's hard to watch Aada suffer, but try to remember to take care of yourself, too."

Eileen had smiled at the therapist with tears in her eyes. "Thanks. You too."

Eileen never did convince Aada to return—not for therapy and certainly not for medication. Without treatment, Aada spent more and more of her days in a world of delusions and conspiracy theories.

That winter, without any hope of getting Aada back into treatment, Eileen made the decision to move on. She could still recall the musty smell of the car as she sat in the driveway watching Aada. Aada was up on the stoop of their townhouse, hair flying in every direction as she frantically installed three more deadbolts. In that moment, Eileen finally understood that her love for Aada wasn't enough to keep them together, to keep Aada safe and healthy. Eileen knew that if she walked up to that house and went inside, she'd risk never getting out. It was like being in a locked cage with a jaguar. She knew her Aada was in there somewhere, but that just made it harder to watch.

That day Eileen put the vehicle in reverse and drove away, leaving behind the life she had built with the woman she loved. It was the hardest thing she'd ever done, and her guilt still burned a hole in her gut, but what else could she have done?

Bzzz, bzzz, bzzz. The alarm on Eileen's phone snapped her back to the present. She felt hot tears running down her cheeks. Silencing her phone, she dismissed the notification that read "30 minutes till class" and dialed.

A voice came across the line: "Dr. Anderson's office, how may I help you?"

"Hi. It's Eileen. Is Dr. Anderson available?"

"One moment please." Then elevator music.

"This is Dr. Anderson, how may I help you?"

"Hi. It's Eileen. Do you have a minute? Something's come up."

"Sure. What's going on?"

9

Fiona tugged on the file wedged beneath the cadaver's foot on her table. She noticed a small impression where the heel had been and ran her fingers across it. It was cold. Fiona opened the file and searched for the sex of the body: Female.

Fiona folded the sheet back to reveal a woman's face and continued reading the police report aloud to her expressionless subject: "Hi there, just going over some details before we begin." Fiona was accustomed to talking to the bodies that came in. They weren't the best conversationalists, but they were better listeners than anyone with a pulse she'd ever met. "It says here you were found on August 17, 2006, in City Hall Park. No ID or identifying documentation was on your person." City Hall Park was notorious for its large homeless encampment. "Mmm, I see."

Fiona looked at the woman's face more closely. A thick layer of dried sweat and dust filled the deep-set wrinkles. "It says here that they guess you're between 40-50 years old." Fiona lifted the lid of the woman's right eye and shone a light into the iris. "Hmmm, I'd say you're closer to 40 than 50, despite your wrinkles."

Typically Fiona was content with the biological indicators of age and physical health at death, but she was feeling particularly curious and decided to dig a little deeper before getting to the autopsy. Fiona walked to her desk where there was a box of the woman's belongings collected from the site. She could smell the pungent odor coming from beneath the lid before she even opened it. Fiona paused and flicked the knob on the hand-held radio sitting on the corner of her desk. "It's *This American Life*. I'm Ira Glass. Today on our program…"

Fiona was lulled into a comfortable flow by Ira's voice as she looked through the box. She lifted each item out one at a time and took an oral inventory. "One pair of grey sweat pants, one T-shirt, one dingy camel-colored trench coat." Fiona squinted to read the faded label. "Prada? Wow. Didn't expect that." She continued the inventory: "One black beanie cap, and one worn-out drawstring backpack." Beneath the bulky clothing sat a plastic specimen bag. Fiona held the bag up to the light and squinted. "And one umbrella in a plastic sleeve with a waterlogged, worn-out birthday card. Fiona double-checked the records taken by the police. At the bottom of the report there was a note about a card "inscribed with the message: 'For Luca on your birthday. Don't leave home without it. Love, Aada.'"

Fiona felt a prickly sensation in the corner of her eyes as she hovered over the words, *Love, Aada.* The handwritten birthday card seemed to breathe life into the woman's body. Fiona struggled to maintain her composure as she imagined the loved ones this woman had left behind.

Fiona's mind drifted to the box of letters tucked under her own bed. They were from her mother, congratulating her on every milestone in her life: birthdays, graduations, anniversaries, there was even one that just celebrated a random Tuesday: "Hi, baby, I just wanted to tell you how proud I am of my baby girl. Know that this Tuesday, and every Tuesday, you're in my heart. Love, Mama. P.S. And all the other days too." Some cards were more precious than others, pliable and soft after being reread hundreds of times. Tear-stained and faded, they were in danger of being read into obscurity.

Fiona wiped back unexpected tears and placed the specimen bag on top of the heap of inventoried items. She tuned into the radio and listened to the woman Ira was interviewing. "He was squatting by the door of local supermarket looking up. And he was asking customers for spare change." Fiona shook her head and cleared her throat. "Now where were we?"

Fiona grabbed her dictaphone and returned to the body. She'd been the city's primary medical examiner for five years now, and she'd learned it was best to keep emotion out of it. It wasn't her nature to be so disassociated, but for the purposes of her job, she found it necessary. A body was a body. Nothing more. Nothing less.

Fiona took the woman's left leg in her hand. She looked over every inch thoroughly. She reported her findings into her dictaphone. "Various moles ranging in size from 1/8 – 1/2 cm." She repeated the procedure on the woman's right leg. "A small birth mark on her right calf. No bruising or abrasions. No lesions." Fiona continued in this way until the entire exterior of the body had been documented. "Nothing medically significant to report on initial inspection. Will continue on to the autopsy." Fiona looked at the woman's face. "Okay, ma'am, the easy part of the exam is complete." Fiona smiled at the body and removed her gloves. She went to her desk and reboxed all the woman's clothing, but left out the plastic bag with the card and umbrella. Fiona opened her laptop and navigated to the report document. She rewound her recordings and started filling out the forms.

Fiona let her mind drift as she typed her notes into the familiar forms. She couldn't help but wonder about this woman's story. *Who are Aada and Luca? Is she Aada? Maybe she's Luca. Maybe she's someone else entirely.* Something about this woman kept Fiona's head busy. Maybe it was the mysterious love note, or the fact the woman had a Prada jacket. Something didn't add up.

Fiona stopped typing and reached for the plastic bag. The crinkling noise was louder than she thought it would be. "Shh!" she scolded the plastic. Fiona looked over her shoulder. Then she gingerly opened the bag and pulled out the greeting card. The paper was soft and pliable, like a pair of perfectly worn-in jeans. She tried to open the card slowly but it was stuck together. Forcing it, a small edge tore. Fiona gasped and looked around her empty lab. *Maybe I should stop*, she thought to herself, but curiosity had taken hold and she pressed on. "For Luca on your birthday," Fiona read aloud.

"Don't leave home without it. Love, Aada." The handwritten message sat humbly beneath the card's stock rhyme. Fiona touched the words written in blue ink.

A segment for NPR's pledge week interrupted Fiona's train of thought. She shut off the radio and scolded herself. "Seriously? Reading dead people's mail? Let's focus, Fiona." She grabbed her dictaphone, snapped her gloves on, donned her face mask and apron, and headed toward the body. "The external examination is complete and now I will begin the autopsy." Her hands moved with familiarity. Her mind drifted in and out of focus, sometimes paying close attention to the body in front of her, other times curious about the various scenarios that may have led to this woman's death.

Fiona opened the chest cavity and moved through each organ. Occasionally she'd take tissue samples for the lab. There were no signs of major disease or infection. The woman was healthy enough, a bit emaciated, but her internal organs were sound.

Fiona was suddenly reminded of the events around her mother's passing. Her mom had been alone in her apartment on the other side of the country. Her body wasn't discovered until she'd missed a few days of work. She'd been in decent health, but was old and had fallen and was unable to get up on her own. With the a/c on high, and no roommate, she'd died of hypothermia, but Fiona thought it would be more accurate to say she died of neglect. Fiona winced at the memory. *Everyone deserves to be remembered well.*

Fiona recorded her findings of the torso and sewed up the body before moving on to the head. She removed the brain for inspection. "There appears to be some bleeding…" —she passed the brain back and forth between her hands— "not sure where from yet. No external abrasion to indicate physical trauma to the head." Fiona grabbed her scalpel and made an incision. "There's an aneurysm sac at the edge of the temporal lobe, about 10 cm in diameter. At some point it ruptured and bled into the rest of the brain. Considering the state of the rest of the body, it can be assumed this was the cause of death." Fiona took a sample of the mass for lab work before placing the brain back in the skull and sealing it up. The samples jars were put in a basket to be picked up by the processing lab. All that was left to do was clean up and finish writing the report.

Fiona took one last look at the woman's face before returning the body to the wall freezer. It looked peaceful, at ease. That's the way Fiona liked remembering all the bodies she worked on: at peace.

"Hello. Is Officer Owens there? It's Fiona. I'm returning her call…" Fiona fiddled with the pen on her desk. It was awkward talking on the phone. She was far more comfortable interacting with her cadavers. Someone came on the line. "Hi, Officer Owens, it's Fiona. You called? … Sure. Can you repeat the name? … Luca?" The card from the woman she'd autopsied a month ago flashed in Fiona's memory. She tried to pay attention to the details Officer Owens was sharing without coming across as flustered. "I see…. Uh-hu…. Thursday? Sure. 4 p.m.? That's fine."

Fiona's heart pounded in her chest as she hung up the phone. She jumped up from her desk and raced to the closet where there were rows of boxed and catalogued belongings of unidentified individuals she'd autopsied. Scanning the case numbers written on the front of each box, she found the one she was looking for. Fiona pulled it off the shelf and placed it on the floor. She was too focused to notice the cramped space as she tore open the lid. On top of a pile of clothing sat a plastic bag with an umbrella and a card inside. Fiona gingerly removed the card from the bag and reread the message for the hundredth time. "To *Luca*. Don't leave home without it. Love, Aada." Fiona sighed. "Luca." A wave of relief washed over her and she felt her eyes well up with happy tears.

Hope was a rare thing in Fiona's line of work. Even in the best-case scenario, she was in constant contact with people who were grieving. But today Fiona felt hope. Someone remembered this woman. Someone cared about her, even in death.

Maybe death isn't the end, Fiona thought to herself. *Perhaps it's a threshold to the next thing, and maybe that next thing can even be connection.*

10

A box of ashes sat at the end of Luca's bed. Life had not gone according to plan, and not just because she had been lying in bed for the better part of a week. Tears filled the small divot in her pillow as she repositioned herself beneath the duvet. Papers and pens, files and clips were tossed to the floor as she tried to get comfortable. Luca felt around under her pillow and pulled out a packet of stapled papers with the city's letterhead. Her chicken scratches, mostly dates, times and phone numbers, filled the borders. Attached to the back was the missing person report she'd filed in June.

Luca remembered how she struggled to fill out the most basic information about her sister. *Jacket: Unknown. Shoes: Unknown. Scars/Marks/Tattoos: Small birthmark on right calf. Last seen: May 2005.* Luca felt guilty about how little she knew about her sister. She hadn't seen Aada in over a year—not much help in a missing persons search. Luca closed her eyes. She could see the autopsy report by the city medical examiner as if it was in front of her. Images of her sister's lifeless face flashed through her mind along with the found handwritten birthday note. "For Luca on your birthday. Don't leave home without it. Love Aada."

Luca screamed at the ceiling. She couldn't decide if she was angry or heartbroken or both. She sat bolt upright in bed. Another cascade of papers tumbled to the floor. Luca frantically rummaged through the mess in front of her. "Where is it? Where is it?!" she mumbled to herself. As finite as the box of ashes at the end of her bed were, Luca still felt unsettled. *Isn't closure supposed to feel better than this?* "Got you!" she said as she grabbed a manila folder out from under a crumpled towel. Luca rifled through the contents until she landed on a handwritten report. At the top was the logo for Virginia Mason Medical Center. "PATIENT COMPLAINED OF HEADACHES, DIZZINESS, AND NAUSEA. CT SCAN WAS ORDERED BUT PATIENT WAS UNCOOPERATIVE AND REFUSED TREATMENT. HAD NO ID. REGISTRATION FORMS LEFT PARTIALLY COMPLETED (SEE ATTACHED). PATIENT DISCHARGED SELF."

Aada had only given her first name to the ER, but they'd taken a blood sample. The city medical examiner cross-referenced her DNA with the open missing person reports and contacted Luca. It was such a surreal experience that Luca still wasn't sure it had actually happened.

Luca shook her head and tried rereading the scant information she had been given. *I must be missing something.* But there was nothing left to tease out of the report. "Ahh!" Luca searched again for the county's medical examiner's autopsy report. "Where are you hiding, Fiona?" Luca had met the woman a week earlier when visiting the morgue to identify

Aada's remains. Fiona had been polite. A bit socially awkward, but it was still nice to talk with someone about her sister. There was something satisfying about sharing stories of Aada with someone who "knew" her, even if it was postmortem.

"There you are!" Luca quickly skimmed the first page and a half of the report. Then she slowed down when she got to the part about Aada's brain. "A HEMORRHAGED ANEURYSM SAC WAS DISCOVERED AT THE EDGE OF THE TEMPORAL LOBE. 10 CM IN DIAMETER. BLOOD ON THE EXTERIOR OF THE BRAIN FOLLOWS A PATH STARTING FROM THE HEMORRHAGE." Flipping to the last page of the report, Luca read the last five words: "CAUSE OF DEATH: NATURAL CAUSES." Luca flopped back onto her pillow. It didn't matter how many times she reread the report, none of it felt real.

Luca's stomach growled. She sat up thinking about food. Her kitchenette was as disheveled as her bed. The tiny counter and sink were full of dirty dishes and half-eaten boxes of cereal and crackers, and her one house plant had wilted and was on the verge of dying. Between the bed where she lay and the kitchenette was a small round table, piled high with clothing, papers and dishes in various stages of cleanliness. Beneath the mess she saw the tip of an umbrella poking out. A new wave of complicated emotions washed over Luca.

Years of anger and hurt bubbled to the surface. Luca was desperate to move on, to come to terms with all that had transpired, but it was proving to be as difficult as untangling a cat from a ball of yarn. Luca couldn't recall any memory or conversation with her sister that didn't conjure up feelings of disappointment, sadness and anger. No memory was untainted by complex emotions. In childhood, Luca had always hoped that her next conversation with her sister would be the one that turned their relationship around. But eventually she came to accept that they'd never be close, and allowed herself to mourn the dream of her and Aada being friends. Once her parents died, all Luca felt was anger.

But after her conversation with Emmy and Jamie about Aada's condition, Luca's overarching emotion toward her sister had been that of concern. And what about the birthday card that was found with her body and addressed to her?

Luca felt burdened. She was the only Talbot left to remember all the family stories, all the recipes, the jokes and the details of vacations gone awry. But she couldn't remember life before elementary school, when Aada was already starting high school. There would be no one telling those stories.

Luca went over the memories of her childhood like running down a shopping list. She hoped that if she kept them in the forefront of her mind, she wouldn't lose them. *The Christmas decorations near the fire place, the time I got stuck in my*

Halloween costume and got scared, Mom's dinner rolls at Thanksgiving, that time when we went camping with Emmy and Jamie…

Luca smiled at the memory of the one and only camping trip they'd ever been on as a family. She had been 7. Aada had been 14 and a full-blown teenager. They were at the beach. Emmy and Jamie had come along, which gave Luca someone to play with since Aada was busy with her music and magazines. The last night they were there, a storm had blown in and tossed their tents around in the wind. At dawn, everyone emerged, sopping wet and grumpy. Emmy had glared at her broken tent, climbed back inside and suddenly sleeping bags and mats, clothing and bags, were flying out of the tent flap. She then emerged and proceeded to gather up what remained of the tent and stormed over to the dumpster. Discovering it was full, Emmy had climbed on top of the heap of garbage, cursing loud enough to wake the entire campground, and started stomping on the pile with her feet. Mom tried to hide her laughter behind cupped hands and dad turned on the car radio full blast. Emmy couldn't help herself. Dancing was in her blood and her grown-up temper tantrum quickly turned into a dance party. Luca remembered how surprised she was to look down and see Aada holding her hand. She was laughing and swinging Luca around in a childish dance. Nothing else in the world existed in that moment except she and Aada. It was all Luca had ever hoped for.

Luca frowned. She couldn't recall what had made Aada walk away so abruptly that day. All she could remember was the hollow feeling she'd felt as she watched Aada slink back to the car.

"Wait!" Luca blurted to the empty room. "Emmy might know." The thought reminded Luca of their recent visit. So much had been revealed about her sister that it was overwhelming. She regretted blaming Emmy. Luca was still really angry, but she wasn't sure it was at Emmy any more, or Aada for that matter. What she wouldn't give to feel safe and loved in one of Emmy's bear hugs. Luca looked at her phone lying next to her. *What would I even say to her?*

Luca's stomach growled again. She knew it was time to venture out into the world and find something to eat, and coffee. She needed coffee. Luca got out of bed. She grabbed a grey hoodie with a big purple W on it and gave it a good sniff. "Clean enough," she said as she pulled it over her head. She stuffed her phone and keys into the front pocket and headed for the apartment door. Luca was so deep in thought that she didn't notice as she laced up mismatched shoes. *I can't just call Emmy after what I said to her. I guess I could apologize, but...* Luca doubled-knotted her right shoe for emphasis. She stood up and headed out the door into the hallway of the building. She paused for a moment to let her eyes adjust to the dim light in the windowless hallway before making her way to the end of the building and to the stairwell leading down to the ground floor.

Luca pulled out her phone and scrolled through her missed calls as she walked. *July 17, 2:45 p.m., Emmy; July 24, 4:00 p.m., Emmy; August 2, 3:01 p.m., Emmy...* The list of ignored calls was growing by the day. Luca scrolled further down, past calls from the police department, her lab and the restaurants she'd ordered take out from. She never knew how lonely a call history could make her feel. She hadn't really considered that her self-isolation would come back to bite her. If anything, it had seemed like an effective way to avoid getting hurt, but now, seeing her utter lack of friends highlighted by the sad state of her call history, she couldn't help but feel she'd made a mistake somewhere along the way.

Luca paused as she reached the top of the stairs leading to the street below. Her thumb hovered over the most recent missed call from Emmy. She took a deep breath. Then, with a tap, the phone began to ring.

Immediately someone picked up. "Luca? Is that you?" Emmy said. In that moment, the sound of Emmy's voice had the same power as her bear hugs.

Luca burst into tears. "Emmy."

"What's going on?!"

Between sobs, Luca explained: "She's gone. Aada's gone."

There was silence on the other end of the line. Then Emmy asked, "Where are you? I'll be right there. It'll be okay."

Luca gave Emmy the address to her apartment and sat down at the top of the stairs. From her vantage point, she could see down to the glass doors that led onto the street. The sidewalk was crowded with people, busy with their own lives, unaware of heartache unfolding just a few feet away.

Luca was suddenly very aware of how exhausted she was. Emmy was the first person, the only person, she had told about Aada, and the relief she felt in sharing the news surprised her. She rested her arms and head on her knees and felt herself falling asleep. She sat up abruptly. *Coffee. I need coffee,* she thought. Luca checked her watch. *It'll probably be another 20 minutes before Emmy arrives.* Outside, ever-growing puddles dotted the wet sidewalk. *Of course it's raining in August.* She pulled the hood up over her head and got to her feet. But something made her hesitate. Something was calling to her.

Luca returned to her apartment and opened the door. She walked over to the table and tossed everything to the floor until the only thing left was the umbrella. She took a deep breath. "Can't forget you." Luca grabbed the umbrella and headed back out. She stepped out onto the sidewalk and let the rain fall onto her head. She knew she had to let go. Let go of her sister, her parents, the missed opportunities and the words left unsaid. Family wasn't like in the movies. It was messy. It was painful. But it was hers. Luca smiled. She popped open the umbrella and headed in the direction of a nearby coffee shop. "Thanks, Aada," she whispered. "For everything."

Acknowledgments

Many thanks to my editor, Ian Cockfield, for helping me become a better writer through the process of completing this book. To my husband, who endured evening after evening discussing imaginary characters as if they were real, and to my brother, Ben, who was the inspiration behind this story.

About The Author

Kate Smithson grew up in the foothills of the Olympic and Rocky Mountains, USA. She believes that everyone's story is important and that we all deserves to be heard. You can read more of her work at anongray.com.

Find Kate online:
anongray.com
Instagram: anon.gray

Did you enjoy this book?

Support indie authors!

Leave a review wherever you purchased this book.
It's one of the best ways to support my work or the work of
any independent author or artist.

Thanks so much!

But wait, there's more!

Download a **free copy** of the short story <u>Lydia</u> that offers a glimpse into Aada's childhood.

Get your copy at www.anongray.com/lydia

An Excerpt From <u>Lydia</u>

Creeeeak. Thud! The ladder came down hard after Lydia pulled the cord. Dust clouds puffed around the open hole in the ceiling.

"Up I go!" Lydia hitched the bucket of soapy water to her elbow and stuffed a bundle of torn-up T-shirts into the string of her apron. "Hello?" she said to the empty space above her. She didn't believe in ghosts, but she thought she'd be polite anyways.